OLLIE'S CHRISTMAS REINDEER

For Jay, Jean, Marion and the original
reindeer girls, Rosie and Raffi.

SIMON AND SCHUSTER
First published in Great Britain in 2016 by Simon and Schuster UK Ltd
1st Floor, 222 Gray's Inn Road, London WC1X 8HB
A CBS Company

Text and illustrations copyright © 2016 Nicola Killen

ISBN: 978-0-85707-600-7 (HB) • ISBN: 978-1-4711-7824-5 (PB)
Printed in China • 10 9 8 7 6 5 4 3 2 1

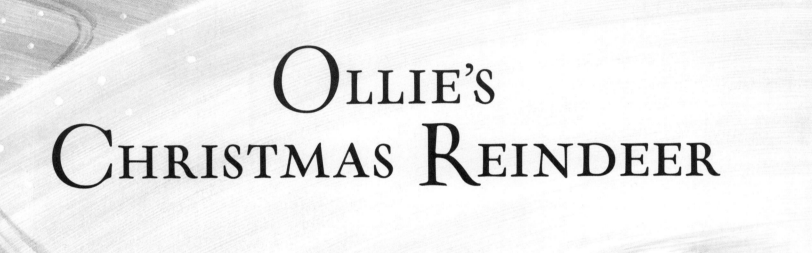

Ollie's Christmas Reindeer

Nicola Killen

SIMON AND SCHUSTER
London New York Sydney Toronto New Delhi

It was Christmas Eve and Ollie had just gone to sleep when

jingle, jingle, jingle

she woke again with a start.

Whooooooosh!

Racing down the hill, she heard the ringing again.

Jingle, jingle, jingle.

And this time it was much clearer.

As the wind whistled and the trees shook, the bells got louder.

Jingle, jingle, jingle.

Ollie was getting close.

She took a deep breath and, feeling very brave,
she ran into the darkness.

There, hanging from a branch,
was a collar circled with silver bells.

Who could it belong to?

Then came a new sound . . .

Crunch, crunch, crunch.

A reindeer stepped through the
crisp snow towards Ollie.

"H . . . h . . . hello," she whispered,
not quite believing her eyes.
"Are you looking for this?"

The reindeer knelt down patiently while Ollie fastened his collar.
Then he lowered himself even further.

Ollie knew exactly what to do and clambered onto his back.
She wondered if they would go for a ride through the forest,
but to her surprise . . .

. . . they soared up into the night sky,
leaving the trees far below!

They travelled over snow-covered
lands and seas glittering in the moonlight.
As they journeyed on, Ollie shivered,
and the reindeer knew there was one last
place he should take her.

The new friends landed softly in the snow. "Thank you," Ollie whispered.

They didn't want to part, but there was someone very special who needed the reindeer's help that night.

Yawning sleepily, Ollie crept back to her room . . .

. . . as her reindeer flew
through the night sky
once more.

In the morning, Ollie found her presents.

Now she would always think of her new friend.
"See you next year!" she whispered.